Red Sled

Patricia Thomas

Illustrated by Chris L. Demarest

BOYDS MILLS PRESS

HONESDALE, PENNSYLVANIA

Text copyright © 2008 by Patricia Thomas
Illustrations copyright © 2008 by Chris L. Demarest
All rights reserved

Boyds Mills Press, Inc.
815 Church Street
Honesdale, Pennsylvania 18431
Printed in China

CIP data is available

First edition
The text of this book is set in 48-point Abobe Caslon.
The illustrations are done in watercolor.
10 9 8 7 6 5 4 3 2 1

For Mallory, Courtney, George, and Clyde—
the newest generation, off to discover the joy of sleds, snow, stars, and books

— *P. T.*

Red sled.

Sad lad.

Sad dad.

Fat hat.

Knit mitt.

Still hill.

Far star.

Snow aglow.

Nighttime climb.

Steep leap.

Slide ride.

Flip-flop
stop.

Roam home.

Hot pot.

Warm-up cup.

Snug hug.

Chin
tucked
in.

Sleepyhead abed.

Flat hat.

Kittens' mittens.

Glad
lad.

Glad
dad.

Red sled.

Author's Note

The structure of this story-poem is inspired by an ancient form of writing called chiasmus (ky-AZ-mus). This format creates a kind of mirror image, with thoughts, words, or even word sounds flowing toward a center point, then reversing to reflect that order as it reaches the end.

In an adaptation of this structure, I've used rhyming pairs—one single, two doubles, and three triples, pivoting on one single rhymed word pair before descending in reverse order. To me, the structure itself formed a "hill," which seemed a good way to tell a story about a father and son sledding.

—P. T.

Red sled.

Sad lad.
Sad dad.

Fat hat.
Knit mitt.

Still hill.
Far star.
Snow aglow.

Nighttime climb.
Steep leap.
Slide ride

Go! Go!
No! No!
Whoa! Whoa!

Flip-flop stop.

Oh my! Eye high!
Snowflake shake.
Giggling wiggling.

Roam home.
Hot pot.
Warm-up cup.

Snug hug.
Chin tucked in.
Sleepyhead abed.

Flat hat
Kittens' mittens.

Glad lad.
Glad dad.

Red sled.